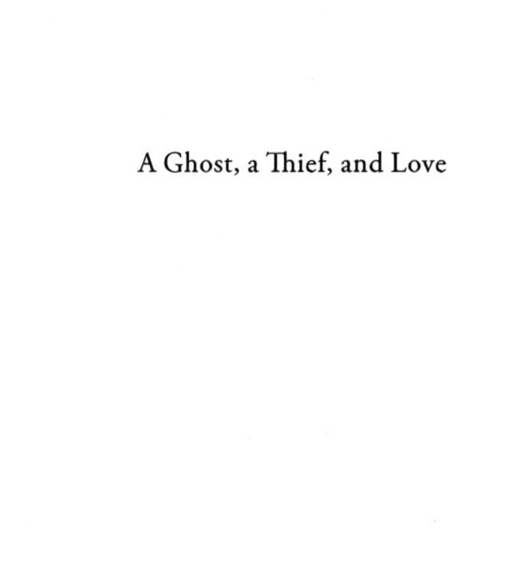

A Ghost, a Thief, and Love

A Ghost, a Thief, and Love

A collection of new poems by Han Jisan
Translated by Lynn Suh

유령, 도둑, 사랑 한지산

K-Poet Series 043
ASIA

Contents

A GHOST, A THIEF, AND LOVE

K

POET

Dancing With a Ghost

Cool white tea and biscuits. Once I'm done
preparing,
a ghost pays a visit.

I wonder, Should I let it lead?
But then I think I ought to show initiative in
the world of the living,
so I make the first move.

As we face each other, I contemplate the next
steps,
but the demanding ghost steps right through
me.

I gently close my eyes
as we play a game of Catch the Thief
to find out who loves the other more.

Thinking that's its cue, the ghost
brings out my inner fears and worries like toys.

I don't really get it.
You tell me how it is since you're the one who's
been hounded by countless hunters.

In this square room,
we're together, yet apart.

In the world of ghosts, they call
a thinker like me a dropout.
I'm a stranger with a face hollowed out,
barely getting loved.

I sweat when I dance.
Doesn't passion belong in the realm of illusion,
not cognition?*

All the doors except the living room's
are dormant.
The two of us are dancing.
Our fingers intertwine, but I'm all alone.

The ghost and the thief are deciphering the
riddle.

* A variation of Alain Finkielkraut's statement in *The Wisdom of Love*: "Since passion is not a matter of cognition, it falls into the realm of illusion."

Pointing to a Bruise

Where does someone like me keep getting hurt?
You laugh awkwardly.

I stroke you with one hand
as if planing wood.

I rub repeatedly with my palm – warmth
  emerges.
No prayer has been said,
but it feels like something has been answered.

Someone like you
sees mind and body
and solid things

as empty spaces*

with see-through eyes.

Evading time, holding its breath,
how does something know what role to play as
soon as it wakes?

Giving white cloth custody

* According to Richard Dawkins' evolutionary perspective, "if humans perceived solid objects as empty space, they would constantly bump into things." (Jack Bowen, *A Journey Through the Landscape of Philosophy*, p. 56)

the wound, trailing after the blue bruise, arrives
  at your door.
The sound of something breaking can be heard
  from inside –
the transparent awl of a god chiseling your body.

What do you pray for?

I just want a place to live in,
see-through and palatable.

When did people start bumping into each other
  anyway?
How is it that after bringing home a god they

discovered,
people griped and wanted to be taxidermied in
a one-off dream?

8×8

Excuse me, I'm looking for a ring.

As you can see, this isn't a lost and found.

If that look was necessary, he was probably just
  doing his job as a guard,

weird as it was, but with that, I spoke up.

Well, I signed up for a reading by my favorite
  author,

and as I sat perusing, strangely enough, only me,

only my voice was out of place,

which persisted till the end.

On my way back from the event, I looked up at
  the sky,

and suddenly, the closer to home I got, I felt
a disconcerting certainty that I might never
make it,
so I threw off everything on me.

I was on the move for half an hour, or an hour,
but it seemed as if others didn't perceive it that
way.
Am I someone stuck in place forever
or going round and round in circles?

One thing's for sure:
I'm a person who can't stand going home alone.
Like a kid, I become

miserable till I'm found, *waah waah.*

You went through adolescence there,
got married, had a child, built a house,
then sent away the grown-up child.

Looking back, there's always
a spot that seems somewhat bare,
like pigeons scattered here and there.

Do you think a housewife, wife, mother, and
 woman
are all the same?
What did God have in mind

when forming a child cleaved from the belly
of a child who was also cleaved from someone's
belly.

While running your hand against concrete, you
said
the world had become a better place, letting us
raise questions like that.
Now I realize it's the not the ring I'm in need of.
First, I need to find myself a home
with someone inside who will say they were
waiting.

I thought you might be dreaming,

or slowly disappearing
because this is a park.
Things keep appearing and disappearing in the park.
Words become disjointed like gibberish –
a one-act play that can't upset anyone since it's short.

In the distance, a whistle can be heard,
like a referee's signaling the end of a match.
She slowly
nods her head.

Returning to my seat, I find her

on a CCTV screen.
A guard's life is security,
and the point of security is life.

In the park,
there are kids who want to play, and kids who
want to be alone,
and kids who watch all of this unfold.

I've decided not to chronicle
the lives of those who've disappeared from the
face of the earth.

The Ripple

The Siamese fighting fish in the fishbowl
won't catch and eat each other.
When one disappears,
the other knows it too will vanish.

By day, they bite;
by night, they embrace and pirouette.

Actually, the Siamese fighting fish don't have
any teeth,
because it doesn't matter who the scales belong
to.

As they bump against the glass,

and bump against the glass,

they shake their little world.

The mouth of the fishbowl is a freefall.

Below Zero

You said you were paying interest,
interest on the money you borrowed for the first time, in college.
It's like endlessly clearing away snow as it's falling,
or like the torture
of putting piping hot water in the freezer expressly to make crystal-clear ice.

And suddenly, with no warning,
it's the feeling of loving someone else, as if loving me.
That's what paying interest is like.

Better not to finish daily tasks in one day,
because they have a domino effect on the
following day and the next.
If that's the case, even in that moment which
has receded so far away from me and become
a mere speck,
a part of you is still on hold, or so I thought.

There are things that occur without being
touched.
Fitted with batteries, a doll can move on its own
and disappear into the distance.
When you first appeared in my dream, my role
was to guard a vault

while unable to say anything, only the wind
    howling in the throat.

What's inside?
I asked.

Well,
there might be nothing at all.
Just a huge vault for me
to sit in front of, alone, full of agitation.
You wanted such a kind of person,

such a role for me.
If I were to come up with the story,

you'd be the one holding the camera –
not a real individual, but someone handing out
  individual roles.
I'm also not the real me here, having brought
  just a shell of myself,
I open it layer by layer –
questions approaching the inner self from the
  outer crust.

It looked unfathomably dreary outside, even
  being with someone, but
we kept at it with our stories, hard though it
  was
not to stare into the void because no one else

arrived.
We exchanged stories

on the staircase landing. It started with
the dream I had last night, but because I don't
dream very often,
let's begin with yours. That dream is usually sad,
absurd
at times, occasionally lovely, and very rarely
a story I want to dream up again. It gets
brought back to life, additionally layered, and
crumpled on our lips.

Hey...! Hey...!

When you call someone's name twice,
it means they're sorely needed,
which is why we spoke each other's names every
once in a while,

in order to become inseparable no matter what,
like how it is with cherished dolls.

I sat in a heated chair. There are those
who doze off all day long right next to a
fascinating story.
There was a time when gentlemen
would hide flowers behind their hats and
present them as surprises.

It's said they did so without thinking twice
about it.

The Invitation

I call someone up. When I get there
no one's home, just a paper cup.

There's a bug inside.
I can't possibly deal with something so
categorically alive.

Can I crumple the cup?
Sure.

If I throw it out, you're going to reappear, right?
Yeah, that's possible.

What if I don't throw it out?

. . . .

Just kidding. I crumple the paper cup
because you're not joking about the bug.

I open the door, throw the cup into the yard,
and turn back.
But I don't hear it fall to the ground.
That's how it sometimes is with things that
weigh very little.

Waiting for you to reappear, I start folding
paper –
a frog, a crane, and recently, I've begun folding

dinosaurs as well.

Things that can't exist and have no reason to
collect in one location
quietly, blindly keep to their places.

A breach, then another.
A yellow, sap-like substance courses down the
wall.

The window frame,
all this effort seems in vain.

An ant crawls in and climbs the white wall.

A listless ant that strayed from its colony.
How brazen will it be?

Can a tree growing close to the window
influence the people inside?

When your day starts with the sound the tree
  makes,
you simply cover your ears and growl, because
  you don't understand it,
or knock the paper cup upside down.

Come to think of it,

isn't this room a confluence of things that can't
communicate?

Looking at the clocks,
each one of them indicates a different hour.
Luckily, I can tell.

We have something in common: we're not able
to read in many languages.
We were communicating with each other in one
of them,

when suddenly,
I wanted to tear off the ant's antenna.

With the signal cut, will the ant's family wander
off

into another language system
like aliens?

Well-folded paper is given a name,
a name based on its appearance,
or does it appear based on what it's named.

Marceline*

Our goal

is to become beautiful,

regardless of age, even as we wilt with time.

Becoming beautiful

has been our one and only wish.

With flair and funk.

* She is a half-human, half-demon vampire character who is one of Finn's friends; Finn is the main character of the American animated television series *Adventure Time.* She is a cross between a human, a demon, and a vampire. She has the nickname "Vampire Queen", as she has killed the Vampire King. She really likes rock music and singing. She turned her family's ax into a bass guitar and goes around playing it. She quietly also has a delicate side, which seems at odds with her laidback, mature image or her impressive strength. She has a tendency to get slightly involved in trivial matters and the reason why her relationship with her father is bad is because he sneakily ate her potato chips. However, a big reason is that ever since turning into a vampire at the age of eighteen, she hasn't matured either physically or mentally.

White

White milk lies asleep
in a vending machine that might or might not
work,
somewhere with a name so plausible
it seems reachable if we try, though far away.

Disguised as a ghost with cobwebs and dust,
if I comply in silence for a while,
I can suddenly get a hold of what I want.

We who made it, who made it through
childhood on vending machines instead of
dairy cows
due to those who didn't know moderation and

exhausted all things white.

The reason why our resentment isn't growing
isn't because we don't dream of falling,
but because our bodies are purging themselves
of whiteness.

Even if it's the same whiteness, what keeps
getting resurrected till before death
is not the same thing as that which expires only
once.

So we compliment those who implant a tooth
even though it costs a pretty penny,

but pluck out premature white hair because it
doesn't look good.

That cycle of reviving one's vitality with white
porridge laid on the table,
after letting black blood from the body

suffering indigestion,
is to fulfill a single role,
mourning those that are born.

Holding a mesh laundry bag, I run the laundry
machine,
whites together with whites,

as if breeding like with like, separate from the
others.

Teeth that were too white rather made us purse
our lips.

An aging neighbor's lips shriveled inward
and I often heard them make a whistling sound,

but in the world turned inside-out
on the drying rack,
a single stain is losing territory,
drying out in all directions.

Didn't the inventor of the laundry machine wish
for loneliness, pure and colorless?

It's not just the laundry machine
whose wailing grows louder as it ages, right?

1 God, 2 Humans,
0 Cups, and Penguins?

There was talk about gods.
Specifically, about a cup that broke
while you were doing the dishes this morning.

Why do cups break without warning?
How could it leave me without saying goodbye?
   What a shame!
Your words clearly had the object in mind,
but did it register them at all? That was
   doubtful.

When the incident occurred, you had to put up
   with another at the same time.
The pickled radish you ordered struck a corner

and all the juiced spilled out from the packet.
Geez, I had no plans to eat any radish today,
but now all of it has to be eaten up before
tomorrow.

Today is a string of bad luck, so I won't step
outside.
Of course, I never do go out. Looking at you,
I say, It's not your fault.
Let's think like the Greeks did.

That's when a god first appeared.
You can think you were forsaken by the Knife
God,

because the cup broke when it hit the heel of a
knife,
and the radish was given the cold shoulder by
the Corner God
when it struck the corner.
All this to say, none of it's your fault.

Gods only turn their backs; I've never seen them
grant any favors!

If gods have never granted any favors to us
humans,
when did we learn to do so?

We stopped talking for a while
and minded our own business.
I pointed out a passage from a book that
resembled your way of talking
and said,

I found a job here you might like,
sending letters from a post office,
but since it's located in Antarctica, it seems
hardly anyone comes to send letters.
Anyway, your task would be
to count penguins.

I wondered what counting them entailed,

and in the book, a character mentioned
   fabricating a number every day.
Say that you saw thirty penguins today,
and tomorrow, exactly seven.
It's about writing up a bogus log every day no
   one checks.

That's me?
Yeah, I laughed because it reminded me of you.

The Magic Chair

If you want to eat breakfast,
fumble your hand along the chair.
The hallway arrives like an ailing traveler.

No matter if it's a four-person room or a six-
person room, you're to use it by yourself.
Even if turning your head sideways
won't make anyone materialize,
every night you're to choose which side to turn
your back to.
When you get up, the side you faced will be all
frumpled up.

An untouched pillow, a deathless cactus,

the palpable anxiety someone feels when
entering a room, even in a dream.

Instead of observing your journey's end getting
closer,
you face the side where the starting line is fading
into the distance.
People call this walking backwards.

When walking backwards, the destination is a
tingling sensation,
your steps faltering along the way.
Beyond the vocal cords' reach, the open sea
coldly installs itself.

I pet the chair for a moment,
it's just outside the door.
You've never been exposed to rain before, huh?
That's just what being a chair's about –

having never absorbed water,
the word 'extract' isn't part of its vocabulary.
But rain vaporizes the past and extracts it.

If that's the case, what about love?
If an era that utterly exhausts love is to come,
we're to place chairs in front of doors and appeal
for sleep.

First, the consonants will disappear,
but the vowels will linger like the pillars of a
temple
and begin to speculate what love is like.

The next day, love will be found on the chair
left behind like provisions.

Even if I live my life duped by something like
magic,
I plan to be a sucker for happiness.

On Such a Fine Day, You

cursed your family. Or
maybe God.

After living in Seoul for just over a year,
you were a wall riddled with holes when you left
the place you lived in.

You walked back home all by yourself,
to that place you loathed. On that day, when
rain was pouring in sheets, your brother and
sister were inside,
but you ended up moving a whole year's worth
of one-person furniture on your own.
When the guy asked if you didn't have a man in

your life,
you said he sounded like a mosquito droning in
your ear.

You wanted to check the weather in Seoul, but
ended up deleting it from your app
You're now no longer there, but want to become
the weather –
a thing people simply accept even when it
conflicts with the forecast.

Can you think of me as a guy?
Maybe that's why you liked the nickname,
Tiger.

On your birthday, I clapped
and belted out "Mountain Hero" at the top of
my lungs.

On the day of Tiger's birthday, everyone came
together,
came together just for you and you alone.

You know, other cars sneak in and park here
illegally.
Decrepit apartment districts merely serve as
parking lots. Saying so,
you conclude that nothing is more harmful than
humans.

Despite the U.S. and China dumping things
illegally,
in the dead of winter, you peel off labels in front
of the recycling area
and add wheat flour to grease drained from
grilling meat
instead of just pouring it out.

You dream of eternal love.
You also want to love discreetly and then give
your body over to a reckless one-night-stand
kind of impulse.
You want to be a man. Strictly speaking, you

don't want to be human.
Even more to the point, you want to see God –
an atheist's final wish.

If you're going to fall sick, I'll come up with a
reason,
and if you want me to name it,
I'll whisper it in your ear, revealing the identity
of the dark secret of life, which seems will last a
lifetime. I'm to eat breakfast with the secret,

as you've just become the weather.

The Altitude of Cultivation

A security guard is on duty five thousand meters
above sea level.
Next to the guard post,
retractable barriers stretch across
a terrain higher than the clouds.

That's right, an apartment building assigns
numbers.
When this child cries, those next-door neighbors
click their tongues,
tsk tsk,
and when the neighbors upstairs stomp around,
the whole night is spent hunting down the
culprit.

Hushing up dog poo and half-eaten ice cream,
why, oh why, is it that night
is more sensitive to voices than to faces?

People on the same horizontal plane are cordial
to each other.
Love spreads from side to side,
disdain from top to bottom.
However, first-floor residents presumably don't
get mad at those who live alone.

While I'm making the rounds delivering bills,
a drunkard reeking of alcohol staggers up to me

five thousand meters above sea level.
Speaking in a mixed tongue, neither Korean nor angelic,
he says he wants to go home.
He comes nearer, waving a basket of fruits in one hand.

He says he went down to sea level, walked around for a short time,
and that people there couldn't have adored him more,
hugging him, kissing him, making a statue in his likeness.
He rambles on as if dreaming.

I gave a shoe to someone I love,
scattered a few buttons into the sea,
and my ID card… my ID card…
His reply circles round the same spot.

I think I can find it
after a few laps around the park.
Walk with me for a little while.
He entices me,
speaking in a mixed tongue that's neither slavish
or demonic.

I hold a flashlight in one hand,

and the drunkard's hand in the other.

What's so nice about that?
The drunkard's hand is warm,
a warmth that can't be felt at five thousand
    meters above sea level.

Walking straight,
then faltering,
just now getting a piggyback ride,

not the guard or the drunkard, but a shadow
reeking of musky body odor.
The few sleepless windows

witnessed it all.

The Small Tournament

In a wide-open space adorned with flags of all
nations, people are gathered.
Clothes emblazoned with figures, business cards
on the ground, soap bubbles,
a lone shoe, all kinds of food and picnic mats.
Take a look around,
members of family units carrying heavy things
in both hands
wander about aimlessly, unable to find a place
to settle.
Whenever a spot was vacated, it was
immediately occupied, but we
found a fairly good spot with a view, settled
down, and readied for the tournament.

We built up our stamina for two months
prepping for today.
We ate eggs and tomatoes, while running and
doing yoga in tandem. Of course,
we didn't neglect spending time with loved ones.
The tournament is so small that the
participating athletes
and their families know each another. Above all,
the vendors in this town
are also its residents. In other words, this
tournament
is very local, spinning in place like that
pinwheel.
It's me, my wife, my wife's younger sister, her

husband, and his relatives.
Generally speaking, it's a family affair.
Smash! A plate shatters.
Two men, both already tipsy, glare at each another.
A gunshot signals the start of the tournament.
An ailing patient watches all of this unfold through the window.
The patient skipped eating soup for breakfast.
The soup would make him fall asleep, and if he were to wake up afterwards,
the entire tournament would be over, with only firework debris scattered on the ground.
When one event concludes, the sweat-drenched

participants collapse and sprawl on picnic mats.
In a secluded spot, someone's vomiting while the town's one public officer pats their back.
The officer is a family member as well, without whom news in the village
would be about a year late. In fact, a festival we organized in the past
was featured in the local newspaper for the first time just this summer.
Finally, like ants bearing food, we all line up in single file
and circle the village. Walking, walking everywhere, every nook and cranny,

looking at each other in the face until there's no
one we don't know left to see.
Cheek to cheek, ear to ear, we say, I love you.
Then we all go back to our separate homes, fall
dead asleep.

The Bouquet

My life is vegetal.

Communicating through walls and curtains,
none
of the laborers showed up for work on the final
day.

The cutting ceremony is nothing special.
Just one more monument littering the ground.

With flower paths leading to and from the
revolving doors,
I made my entrance like a fairy tale,

like a tendril stretching towards the lake.

It's very easy
to bring me down.

Humans are pliable like rubber.
Humans consist of bones and water.
Humans disintegrate because of water.

After pressing our faces into each other's hand,
we haven't seen each other since.
Loved ones are always farthest from me.

Due to those who can't pay their debts,

I stretched out my tendrils and thrust them in
all directions, from the ground to the clouds.

Dark clouds clustered high in the sky,
and in the lower regions, light – to be collected
– spread.

When a thief broke in,
I extended my arms.

The thief removed his mask and struck up a
conversation with third parties.
We're accomplices, he said.

When the curtain lifted, we gathered the edges
of weatherworn faces,
paring and pruning them until they formed into
a vase.

Someone enters a flower shop and strikes up a
conversation.
There's someone I'd like to encourage. Is there a
nice flowery word I can use?

Giving flowers is in and of itself giving
encouragement.

The florist cuts along the perforated line,

and holding the scissors
divulges how to achieve longevity.

Did you know that plants communicate
through walls and curtains?
So, every single bouquet is a letter.

The stems, the wrapping, the ribbons
are tied together.

The eyes are about to flee.

The Patient

In ancient Africa,
there was a tribe of headless people.
With facial features on their chests,
their hearts lay behind their expressions.
Their descendants are nowhere to be found.

I relate this and other
stories to him.

About how to grip a curve ball.
There were ten players; each of them had a
different grip.
The balls fell the same way, though they each
traced a different arc.

Someone steps onto the field.
Slide, then another slide.
The way home is slippery
and the bases free.

He gazed at where I was gazing,
and peered deeper into the distance.

What I'm capable of doing is
falling in love again, though languishing from a
serious illness,
though it smiles and makes its rounds, infecting
and spreading.

As soon as I wave my hand, everyone stares.
My body's illuminated.

I'm growing light as day,
heavily pressed like a flattened flower. I hope
he holds onto me, with an iron grip.

He arrives,
like a fallen leaf,

to revive the boxer who's been knocked
  unconscious.
Like a referee lunging forward,
I'm already heading out to meet him.

The Shell in the Wasteland

A woman is sitting on a bench
next to a bicycle with a basket, the kind she
  long wanted to have.
How've you been?
she asks, facing the lake where the far shore
is visible. It takes roughly 40 minutes for a
  grown man
to walk around this lake.
The trees have absorbed time differently, each in
  its own way,
sprouting leaves of different colors from the
  same roots.
We are each other's guests from far away:
me a guest from the west, she a guest from the

east.

Sitting on an ownerless bench makes the heart
flutter.

Green can brighten without any lighting
at 2PM. Gazing at the nearest color, she asks,
Do you still like botanical gardens?
Deep blue is the color. Her gaze grasps
something like a pair of tweezers.
This is the hardest place to track the weather.
After coming back from on an unforgettable
trip, she put a slender ring on her finger
and traversed time–an hour and a half.
Skipping over rivers, hopping over lights,
bounding past steering wheel and traffic

lights,
we exchange big and small talk. We guide each
other.
When one of us experiences emotional distress,
the other extends their hand.
When one of us loses their footing, we stop in
our tracks.
It's worrying to hear
you're on strong medication.
She's been growing weak twice a day, morning
and evening,
and is that much more cautious,
like a mountain lord who's lost their land to an
all-consuming fire.

Despite that, she pulls out two fairly large
  tangerines
from her basket and hands one to me.
At that very moment, she see me for the first
  time.
We've exalted different miseries in different parts
  of the world –
I, the misery of certainty, she, the misery of
  uncertainty.
Much later,
our stories remove to the mountains.
We both agree
and become barefoot, treading on peeled strips
  of bark.

Black eyes morph into dark trees.

Our fellowship

has only lasted a hundred years,

laughing, crying, writing and discarding.

Will a night hiker

be able to recognize that this was once a bench?

Responses to greetings

and recent events

are the first to rot, becoming compost,

layering stories on stories.

The scent of tangerines,

making every corner of the forest redolent with it,

is proof that we inhabited the same time zone.

Move-in Cleaning

I hire someone.

I, too, can clean out what's visible to the naked eye.

What I really want

is for the vocal cords of this house to resemble
  mine,

so that it can cry even when I'm not here.

It took more than twenty years

to replace my previous home with this one.

Like an organism risking its life in the process of
  molting,

I moved here just barely holding onto my one

and only life.

Even in the midst of family disagreement, each one of us
stoically eats breakfast and goes to work.

A bug full of curiosity stumbles upon this house
and invites its whole family. At the tail end of this,
there's a certain sweetness.

They too are creatures that stretch out their bodies and sleep.

The underground dwelling I'll inhabit one day
might also be exhibited
as material evidence of a certain lifestyle in the
far future.

A thought pops into my head:

Can a skull represent a household economy?
Can paper professionally shed its skin over and
over again?

Moisture stirs in different rooms by turns,
to prove it's not me that's wrong with the
picture here.

The floor can be covered with linoleum.
I can also put on clothes
as a member of a generation that wears clothes
with no frills.
So, life
is the *I* that remains after the feathers have been
plucked and the leather peeled.

That *I*
only seems to be a bother now,
so I leave, laundry basket in hand,
and just like that, I was about to make for the
distance,

but ended up waiting absentmindedly
in front of a laundry machine,
because its eye resembles the eye of one
doing something slowly and for a long time.

When the world's noisy spin cycle ends,
I end up looking for fruit or water or the like.

I wasn't sure if the room had whitened
or if noon had arrived,
because I'm no professional in this field.

Sweating and smiling, they open the door.

We're all done here, come in and see
if we can leave, with your permission of course.

Good bye!
Please clean the other homes just like you did
here,

if you guys are more or less solely responsible for
the move-in cleaning in this area.

What the Coin Does

Lies down, then gets back up again.
Not me, but the arcade game character.
With a single coin, the person lying down got
back up.

Crossing an overpass with friends, our
commotion
was noising past a person in a wheelchair.
Someone from our crowd
shook out all the coins in his pocket. He was
catching up to us
when he went off somewhere, just like a coin
that falls out.

One day, when I was walking by the overpass,
there was a vendor selling saplings.
Word has it, if you go plant a leg in the forest,
it can stand upright forever. So,
at night, the forest
will stroll into the neighborhood.

Claiming that meeting up at night than in the
daytime leaves a more lasting memory,
our time together darkened as if descending the
staircase to the basement.
Night always wore a face as if hiding something,
so we dug beneath the tree.
Finding nothing, we buried what could be

found later.

We kept inserting coins.
The night stood up, and kept standing.

The tree had made thousands of prayer rooms
in each of its roots,
but only one hand could find entrance to my
pocket,
so I quietly went in alone.
I plunged in my hand
until the black sky appeared like a black screen.

With each step we took, we heard the coins

clenching their fists and clashing
over an ending we didn't know.
To view the noise,
the forest gathered around us.
Paths, more numerous than the day, confused
us.

We shook out all our coins, got up, and went
our separate ways.
When someone says goodbye and disappears,
it seems like they're going somewhere unknown
to us.
Arriving in their own neighborhood,
meeting someone in a mysterious spot,

it seems like they would smile and say, today
was a good day.

In the back of the arcade cabinet screen,
it seems like they would gently touch those
spots where they struck each other.

Light Speed

That which would have depth, width, and height. Crafted by humans. Satisfying to all. To both humans and things. I get width and height. But what about depth? The surrounding circumstances? Background history? This home has had several reported incidents, something I heard about before I purchased it, but it didn't influence my decision. Not exaggerating is your virtue, being mild-mannered is mine. Accordingly, this house remains a mystery, existing just in photos, videos, and in the past. You looked at someone when there was a problem, wanting them to solve it without you saying so, with the attitude that they would understand your plight. Right, attitude's important. It's like underfloor heating, which plays the most critical role in floor construction, because we're people who, sooner or later, have to live with our feet to the ground. If it's cold, where can we put our feet? Even birds that fly lean on branches on an island somewhere, but we have nowhere to lean on at all, which is why I went ahead with the purchase. Surely there are places where people like us live, right? Don't you want to quit living in a low-income, low-rise neighborhood or an area where murder happens every once in a while? I wanted to move out. If possible, I even wanted to take off my name and surname, leaving them behind in my hometown. When a person transforms into the speed of light, word has it that they lose their reflection in the mirror. That feels true, but it's hard to make sense of it. Do you want to take the form of light? Yes, I do. I take out a single incandescent bulb and show you its filament. So you're saying you can step inside and live in here. Of course I can, I can live in a very small space or in very large one. As long as width × length × height are given, as long as empty space isn't wasted as a resting place for the gaze to lounge around in.

You're not confined by roles. Sometimes you

put on your apron backwards or watch family movies alone. You're lenient towards murderers and express disapproval at new schools of thought. You work quickly, *chop-chop*. The doorbell has rung several times. Once it was the neighbor checking if anyone was home; once it was the police. This home has had several reported incidents in the past. It exists in your memory, in your mirror.

Not as light, but something like it.

Narration

I lift the toilet seat lid and urinate.
Outside the window, it's a pale yellow.
A reply to my inquiry has arrived by email.
It says the company's not at fault.

It's the beginning of autumn.
Once the season of decay arrives,

things falling
are so cheap and fragile,
they're easy to scoop up and mock.

Just outside the door, grandma shouts.
A pigeon has torn open the trash bag again.

Pigeons fly away when spoken to.
Standing where I am, I receive the brunt of
grandma's rage.

I prepared to boil cherry tomatoes.
I scored them crosswise.
Nothing for guests,
no one's a guest.

There are those who dislike pigeons
and those who say they hate their grandmas,
barking puppies, and the puppies' pleading
owners.

Cherry tomatoes start floating up.
Is it because, no matter what we say, we don't
understand each other
if our aims diverge?

Floating to the surface of the sea, the fish
didn't even care to regard people in any way.
Only those who don't put on scuba gear are
truly free.
Where freedom overflows,
the living and the dead rise to the surface
together.

The security guard laying rat poison

and the person stacking dirty dishes in the
alleyway
weren't playing hide-and-seek.
It can't be hide-and-seek
when you put your mind and body into it.

They say one can hear something speak
in artfully taken photos.
This neighborhood was like that too.
There wasn't a soul in sight, but I could hear
something spoken.

Opening my window, the scent puffed by the
house across from us circulated.

It was smoking something good.
A fragrance that shouldn't belong in the home
lingered.
It made me feel so awkward

that I read a book, though no one paid
attention.
While I read it, it made sense,
but when I finished reading, my mind went
blank.
I mean, the next day forgetting the day before
is such an obvious thing,
it's the oppression
of being forced to recall nothing.

A cat stretched out its body
and crouched on the floor.
It hopped onto a fence
and vanished somewhere beyond my reach in a
blink of an eye.

When absurdities happened
so matter-of-factly,
mom clicked her tongue and said it was the end
times.
The end times could conveniently describe
anything.

The end times if I didn't win the lottery.
The end times if today's meal was bland.
The end times if my friend forgot my birthday.
The end times were fragile.
The end times persisted,
latching onto me, even after I came home, even
in my dreams.

Next Saturday, I've got a job interview,
but I can't make out the thoughts of the person
in the mirror.
He went through his motions in the bathroom.

After plucking out his facial hair one by one

with tweezers,
he took a shower, and cleaned the mold from
the walls and the floor.
Afterward, he took a huge dump, contentment
writ large on his face,
stood up and slowly danced
a dance which certain books forbid.

Then he sat and stood up over and over again,
leaving footprints, butt-naked.

POET'S NOTE

1 = 0.9999999

When I want to say something.

I set about talking about a chair in the room for example. Usually this is how:

1. Describing the chair as precisely as possible.
2. Describing everything in the room except for the chair.

Both methods start with observation. Either by intently focusing or thoroughly evading the subject of description. The former grants what is to be depicted a strong sense of gravity. With both feet on the ground, there's no anxiety. But also no wings. The latter is dispersal. It's an intentional exercise of distancing oneself from what is to be shown. Distance of evasion = distance of concern. When the object loses its importance, the gaze returns to where the observation initially began. My writing is a continuum of describing and evading.

A Ghost, a Thief, and Love divides a single word into thirds. That word never once appears in the poetry collection. I brought in a ghost, a thief, and love to explain it. Describing these three words became a form of evasion. I concluded the poetry collection without ever conclusively saying what I meant. This collection adheres to life. The poems are linked to characters, settings, and events, but the poems don't merge with them. They accompany each other, but don't meet; they are conscious of each other, but don't invite the other. Like how people continue to gaze at the sky, look at the forest, and cry where no one's there – absence can be a way of proving presence.

Is it a positive or negative thing that completing a poem obstructs writing the next. They say a collection should contain completed pieces that, when viewed together, convey something that permeates through all of them – is that something I possess or something someone is to give. I am constantly looking for a place to stand, like a figure emerging on the third riverbank. When one poem overflows itself, it's as though the next poem should somehow be diminished for that reason. But poetry is just poetry, no more, no less. The same goes for meaning. Meaning is just meaning, like how someone's first-place priority might be someone else's fourth or fifth.

At times, I feel as though I'm doing well. I've never made a huge enemy of anyone, I owe only debts I can manage, and I have a place to sleep without having to be mindful of others. That's to say, in my daily life, at least, nothing unsettles me. But poetry is something different. All manner of things unsettle me. Poetry even regards me as an object – a profoundly fair treatment. If life is confession or problem-solving, then poetry is like roulette or the lottery. Though I'm the one writing, sometimes the poem becomes an independent entity, while I become reliant upon it. I'm a person who pulls a lever every day. There are countless others next to me pulling theirs; the person seated at the far end is me, or you perhaps.

There were poems completed before I ever began writing them. Some were written with someone strongly in mind. Others were born from conversation, from a thought, from worry, or from anger. Looking at them, it feels like I've entered a dance competition (where I'm to bring a partner) all alone. My partner was assuredly beside me, but only my name is on the list. I'm embarrassed and grateful. Looking out from the spotlight, I want to go back to the other side, to where they are, the people I love.

I leave untouched the remaining 0.1.

POET'S ESSAY

K

POET

A Notes Exhibition

1/1/2024

“It’s charming when we realize that a figure who has a feature we yearn for resembles us.”

It’s tedious, isn’t it? Coming back to the beginning; after a lifetime of walking, arriving here as the final destination.

2/3/2024

When change is in the air, some species feel an overwhelming urge to migrate. This is known as *Zugunruhe*.

2/4/2024

Snipping one act of forgiveness into thin strips.
Thus, you live a lifetime of atonement.

2/10/2024

Error

I'm awake, but there's no movement.
I'm tired of gazing at the same place,
the immutability of yesterday and today, and me, happening to no one but myself.

2/22/2024

When it snows, no petitions are submitted.

Good breathing makes good posture.

An upright posture sustains me.

4/29/2024

I bought two lottery tickets.
This doesn't mean I've doubled my chances of winning.

I'm keeping one
and giving the other to someone I like,
but that person
hates gambling, or more precisely, hates being reliant on anything.

5/11/2024

Naming a sorrow.

The clothing rack collapsed.

Can even one person become a floor?

6/9/2024

Disposition and inertia.

Dreams don't begin on page one,
but leave marks where they've landed like bombshells.
When we wake, we fumble through ourselves
just as we blindly feel for those traces.

Each time I give up a course of action, stooping over and folding my legs, a seed is planted.

6/21/2024

Swinging an electric fly swatter,
sparks fly on a long summer night

while it's snowing in Mongolia.

6/23/2024

Stuttering is akin
to being submerged in water.

7/9/2024

It seems like the word *borrow* is vanishing as of late.

It's either *own* or *give*.

Just dropping by to return something is excessive now.

7/21/2024

The advantage of time travel is

I can outpace my last will

left for those who don't know where to go.

Life is

1. a linear route: past-present-future
2. a circular route: spring-summer-fall-winter.

7/28/2024

I watched a low-budget play.

You were my
senior, then my junior,
then a distant ancestor,
then my enemy.

You must've had a hard time. But,
it was possible because of you. It had to be you.
No one else wanted to do it.

8/14/2024

The next world.

A world without you.
Once you became all things in this world,

only then was I unable to see you.

9/3/2024

Letters are nothing but ice.

From left to right,
from top to bottom.

When they melt,
they become mere sentiments.

9/8/2028

Because I've become the disagreeable angst of an era,
like an old, unsolved case.

9/12/2024

I don't know why,
but I like you.

9/18/2024

After the movie ended, I said,
Wasn't the color of the trumpet creeper beautiful?
The movie was in black and white,
she said.

COMMENTARY

Towards an End Pointed to by Obscure Fragments

Heo Hee (Literary Critic)

Every day, as we make decisions, we hope they bring the intended results. However, reality often turns out to be quite different from our expectations. Life constantly veers unpredictably. We exist with the perpetual anxiety of uncertainty – who can truly be free from such a burden? *A Ghost, a Thief, and Love* presents snapshots of those who journey towards an unknown conclusion. Perhaps, as this collection of poetry suggests, it is precisely because we do not know the outcome of the events we face that we manage to keep living. In a transparent world where everything follows a predetermined path, we might, in fact, lose the sense of life's meaning more easily. For Han Jisan's poetic speaker, the meaning of life is not a given; it is something to be found among unknown fragments in the midst of coincidence.

Take the poem "Below Zero." The line, "Better not to finish daily tasks in one day, / because they have a domino effect on the following day and the next," depicts the poetic self navigating through and redefining itself across the boundaries of segmented time. We typically perceive time in an organized fashion, where work ends and a new day begins, but this poem clearly points out that time does not divide so neatly. What happens today impacts tomorrow, and what happens tomorrow influences today. This interwoven flow of time, unpredictably affecting us, feels undeniably true for nearly everyone. Faced with an uncontrollable environment shaped by time, individuals are led into the process of rediscovering themselves. This is a hallmark of the ontological dimension in Han Jisan's poetry.

"Dancing With a Ghost" depicts a poetic self at the threshold of reality and illusion, life and death. It faces the world beyond this one and tries to take the lead, as seen in the following lines: "I wonder, Should I let it lead? / But then I think I ought to show initiative in the world of the living, / so I make the first move." The line "but the demanding ghost steps right through me" reveals that this attempt does not go smoothly. The ghost is not an illusion, but represents the unavoidable domain of uncontrollable complexity that the poetic self encounters. Through the process of dancing with the ghost, the poem emphasizes that one's self cannot be established alone. Interestingly, the poetic self perceives this interaction as an aspect of love: "we're… together, yet worlds apart," reflecting a kind of connection imbued with failure or indeterminacy.

The exploration continues in "The Ripple." The lines, "The Siamese fighting fish in the fishbowl / won't catch and eat the other. / When one disappears, / the other knows it too will vanish," point to the intimate nature of interdependent relationships. Their coexistence is not for each other's sake; rather, there is an instinctive sense of crisis – that if one disappears, the other cannot endure the loss. The fear that swallowing the other will ultimately lead to oneself being swallowed by something reinforces the importance of coexistence. This "something" is not a tangible entity but rather the effect of isolation and loneliness. Nevertheless, the symbiotic relationship between the two fish can still be seen as an expression of love, with a fundamental sense of motion, a tremor inherent in their relationship.

This motion is also expressed outwardly: "as they bump against the glass, / and bump against the glass, // they shake their little world." Bumping on the glass is both a struggle to escape a rigid world and a process of more firmly recognizing the other. Additionally, the poem highlights that love involves inevitable tension and fault-lines rather than a state of perpetual peace. Paradoxically, love deepens through such extremities. Han Jisan's poetic understanding of 'the wisdom of love', as seen in "Dancing With a Ghost", reflects this perspective. Another example is in the spatially nuanced lines from "The Altitude of Cultivation": "People on the same horizontal plane are cordial to each other. / Love spreads side to side, / disdain from top to bottom." The poet does not emphasize any romantic notions of love, but rather the horizontal expansion of love contrasted with the vertical hierarchy of disdain, embodying the wisdom of love that this poetry collection seeks to convey.

At this point, it is worth noting again that

Han Jisan's poetry does not remain confined to a metaphysical state comprised of abstract concepts. In this collection, the vivid details of workers struggling at their jobs, such as "security guards" and "delivery people" are clearly present. It portrays the hardships and fears of those fighting to make a living, as captured in a passage from "Coexistence": "You couldn't escape from under the shadow of the rainbow parasol until all the fried chicken was sold; in the day, you were dying of heat, and at night, you trembled with fear of there being leftovers." Today's violence on the world stage is also referenced in such lines as "the night when Israelis massacre Palestinians," and is also connected to the fate of migrant workers in "The Tragedy of Migrant Workers", who are forced to live as if they were "not in a continuum of life / but starting again from broken pieces." The uncertainty and contemplation of boundaries that characterize Han Jisan's poetry are grounded in real life, rather than in virtual thought experiments.

In this light, it seems only natural that Han Jisan was chosen as the recipient of the 2024 Sim Hun Literary Award, an award honoring writers rooted in real life, regardless of the genre they write in. In A Ghost, a Thief, and Love, he does not simply convey resignation over having to live precariously without knowing the end. Instead, he reminds us that unexpected events can open new pathways. Knowing the outcome is not important. The only proposition we must understand is that the end is unknowable, and the insight we must gain is that life cannot be a game of piecing together a predetermined conclusion. The truly significant value lies in each moment when we choose the unknown, in focusing on how the fragments that emerge from those choices transform us. This is the testimony of Han's poetry collection.

PRAISE FOR HAN JISAN

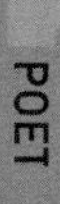

In works like "Mourning by Myself" and "Pointing to a Bruise", Han Jisan's tenacity stands out as he seizes control of the message and builds poetic validity on his own, free from rigid structures, while imploding the limitations of expression. His steady rhythm, the rhythmic layering, and the strategic variations on thematic urgency are also remarkable. Above all, the persistence and strength to flesh out his own poetic world as a young poet, while gratifying our "expectation of originality" has earned him high marks.

–From the judges' comments for the 2021
Munhaksasang Newcomer Literary Award
(Judges: Kwon Yeongmin, Mun Hyewon, Shin Dong-ok)

The work "Below Zero" depicts a situation and weaves a narrative in a minus state (below zero), employing various images to present a montage-like portrayal of modern lives unable to achieve existential self-realization. Along with "Dancing With a Ghost" and "The Bouquet", "Below Zero", in particular, offers insightful and apocalyptic visions of contemporary subjects who cannot live as autonomous beings, revealing the structural forces in the world that perpetuate such conditions.

–Hwang Chibok, "Languages Living in an Uncertain Era" (*Yeolinsihak*, Spring 2023)

"The Altitude of Cultivation" and 51 other poems explore the hidden dimensions of existence in everyday objects and fractured landscapes, creating a poetic space at the boundary of reality and idealism. Particularly in "The Altitude of Cultivation", the opening line, "a security guard is on duty five thousand meters above sea level," conjures up an extreme terrain and leads the reader to a surreal scene, overturning the conventional concept of everyday space while revealing the multifaceted properties inherent within it. The image of a security guard working "higher than the clouds" is fantastical and yet oddly reflective of reality. Such imagination not only crosses the boundaries of space but also serves as a metaphor for the social and psychological boundaries that we do not fully grasp. Additionally, this collection is highly regarded for maintaining a consistent poetic exploration with balance and cohesion throughout.

–From the judges' comments for the 2024 Sim Hun Literary Award (Judges: Kim Keun, Ahn Hyun-mi, Heo Hee)

K-POET

A Ghost, a Thief, and Love

Written by Han Jisan
Translated by Lynn Suh
Published by ASIA Publishers
Address 445, Hoedong-gil, Paju-si, Gyeonggi-do, Korea
(Seoul Office: 161-1, Seodal-ro, Dongjak-gu,Seoul, Korea)
Email bookasia@hanmail.net
ISBN 979-11-5662-317-5 (set) | 979-11-5662-726-5 (04810)
First published in Korea by ASIA Publishers 2024

*This book is published with the support of the Literature Translation Institute of Korea (LTI Korea).

바이링궐 에디션 한국 대표 소설

한국문학의 가장 중요하고 첨예한 문제의식을 가진 작가들의 대표작을 주제별로 선정!
하버드 한국학 연구원 및 세계 각국의 한국문학 전문 번역진이 참여한 번역 시리즈!
미국 하버드대학교와 컬럼비아대학교 동아시아학과, 캐나다 브리티시컬럼비아대학교 아시아학과 등 해외 대학에서 교재로 채택!

바이링궐 에디션 한국 대표 소설 set 1

분단 Division

01 병신과 머저리-**이청준** The Wounded-**Yi Cheong-jun**
02 어둠의 혼-**김원일** Soul of Darkness-**Kim Won-il**
03 순이삼촌-**현기영** Sun-i Samch'on-**Hyun Ki-young**
04 엄마의 말뚝 1-**박완서** Mother's Stake I-**Park Wan-suh**
05 유형의 땅-**조정래** The Land of the Banished-**Jo Jung-rae**

산업화 Industrialization

06 무진기행-**김승옥** Record of a Journey to Mujin-**Kim Seung-ok**
07 삼포 가는 길-**황석영** The Road to Sampo-**Hwang Sok-yong**
08 아홉 켤레의 구두로 남은 사내-**윤흥길** The Man Who Was Left as Nine Pairs of Shoes-**Yun Heung-gil**
09 돌아온 우리의 친구-**신상웅** Our Friend's Homecoming-**Shin Sang-ung**
10 원미동 시인-**양귀자** The Poet of Wŏnmi-dong-**Yang Kwi-ja**

여성 Women

11 중국인 거리-**오정희** Chinatown-**Oh Jung-hee**
12 풍금이 있던 자리-**신경숙** The Place Where the Harmonium Was-**Shin Kyung-sook**
13 하나코는 없다-**최윤** The Last of Hanak'o-**Ch'oe Yun**
14 인간에 대한 예의-**공지영** Human Decency-**Gong Ji-young**
15 빈처-**은희경** Poor Man's Wife-**Eun Hee-kyung**

바이링궐 에디션 한국 대표 소설 set 2

자유 Liberty

16 필론의 돼지-**이문열** Pilon's Pig-**Yi Mun-yol**
17 슬로우 불릿-**이대환** Slow Bullet-**Lee Dae-hwan**
18 직선과 독가스-**임철우** Straight Lines and Poison Gas-**Lim Chul-woo**
19 깃발-**홍희담** The Flag-**Hong Hee-dam**
20 새벽 출정-**방현석** Off to Battle at Dawn-**Bang Hyeon-seok**

사랑과 연애 Love and Love Affairs

21 별을 사랑하는 마음으로-**윤후명** With the Love for the Stars-**Yun Hu-myong**
22 목련공원-**이승우** Magnolia Park-**Lee Seung-u**
23 칼에 찔린 자국-**김인숙** Stab-**Kim In-suk**
24 회복하는 인간-**한강** Convalescence-**Han Kang**
25 트렁크-**정이현** In the Trunk-**Jeong Yi-hyun**

남과 북 South and North

26 판문점-**이호철** Panmunjom-**Yi Ho-chol**
27 수난 이대-**하근찬** The Suffering of Two Generations-**Ha Geun-chan**
28 분지-**남정현** Land of Excrement-**Nam Jung-hyun**
29 봄 실상사-**정도상** Spring at Silsangsa Temple-**Jeong Do-sang**
30 은행나무 사랑-**김하기** Gingko Love-**Kim Ha-kee**

바이링궐 에디션 한국 대표 소설 set 3

서울 Seoul

31 눈사람 속의 검은 항아리-**김소진** The Dark Jar within the Snowman-**Kim So-jin**
32 오후, 가로지르다-**하성란** Traversing Afternoon-**Ha Seong-nan**
33 나는 봉천동에 산다-**조경란** I Live in Bongcheon-dong-**Jo Kyung-ran**
34 그렇습니까? 기린입니다-**박민규** Is That So? I'm A Giraffe-**Park Min-gyu**
35 성탄특선-**김애란** Christmas Specials-**Kim Ae-ran**

전통 Tradition

36 무자년의 가을 사흘-**서정인** Three Days of Autumn, 1948-**Su Jung-in**
37 유자소전-**이문구** A Brief Biography of Yuja-**Yi Mun-gu**
38 향기로운 우물 이야기-**박범신** The Fragrant Well-**Park Bum-shin**
39 월행-**송기원** A Journey under the Moonlight-**Song Ki-won**
40 협죽도 그늘 아래-**성석제** In the Shade of the Oleander-**Song Sok-ze**

아방가르드 Avant-garde

41 아겔다마-**박상륭** Akeldama-**Park Sang-ryoong**
42 내 영혼의 우물-**최인석** A Well in My Soul-**Choi In-seok**
43 당신에 대해서-**이인성** On You-**Yi In-seong**
44 회색 時-**배수아** Time In Gray-**Bae Su-ah**
45 브라운 부인-**정영문** Mrs. Brown-**Jung Young-moon**

바이링궐 에디션 한국 대표 소설 set 4

디아스포라 Diaspora

46 속옷-**김남일** Underwear-**Kim Nam-il**
47 상하이에 두고 온 사람들-**공선옥** People I Left in Shanghai-**Gong Sun-ok**
48 모두에게 복된 새해-**김연수** Happy New Year to Everyone-**Kim Yeon-su**
49 코끼리-**김재영** The Elephant-**Kim Jae-young**
50 먼지별-**이경** Dust Star-**Lee Kyung**

가족 Family

51 혜자의 눈꽃-**천승세** Hye-ja's Snow-Flowers-**Chun Seung-sei**
52 아베의 가족-**전상국** Ahbe's Family-**Jeon Sang-guk**
53 문 앞에서-**이동하** Outside the Door-**Lee Dong-ha**
54 그리고, 축제-**이혜경** And Then the Festival-**Lee Hye-kyung**
55 봄밤-**권여선** Spring Night-**Kwon Yeo-sun**

유머 Humor

56 오늘의 운세-**한창훈** Today's Fortune-**Han Chang-hoon**
57 새-**전성태** Bird-**Jeon Sung-tae**
58 밀수록 다시 가까워지는-**이기호** So Far, and Yet So Near-**Lee Ki-ho**
59 유리방패-**김중혁** The Glass Shield-**Kim Jung-hyuk**
60 전당포를 찾아서-**김종광** The Pawnshop Chase-**Kim Chong-kwang**

바이링궐 에디션 한국 대표 소설 set 5

관계 Relationship

61 도둑견습 – **김주영** Robbery Training-**Kim Joo-young**
62 사랑하라, 희망 없이 – **윤영수** Love, Hopelessly-**Yun Young-su**
63 봄날 오후, 과부 셋 – **정지아** Spring Afternoon, Three Widows-**Jeong Ji-a**
64 유턴 지점에 보물지도를 묻다 - **윤성희** Burying a Treasure Map at the U-turn-**Yoon Sung-hee**
65 쁘이거나 쯔이거나 - **백가흠** Puy, Thuy, Whatever-**Paik Ga-huim**

일상의 발견 Discovering Everyday Life

66 나는 음식이다 – **오수연** I Am Food-**Oh Soo-yeon**
67 트럭 – **강영숙** Truck-**Kang Young-sook**
68 통조림 공장 - **편혜영** The Canning Factory-**Pyun Hye-young**
69 꽃 – **부희령** Flowers-**Pu Hee-ryoung**
70 피의일요일 – **윤이형** BloodySunday-**Yun I-hyeong**

금기와 욕망 Taboo and Desire

71 북소리 - **송영** Drumbeat-**Song Yong**
72 발칸의 장미를 내게 주었네 - **정미경** He Gave Me Roses of the Balkans-**Jung Mi-kyung**
73 아무도 돌아오지 않는 밤 – **김숨** The Night Nobody Returns Home-**Kim Soom**
74 젓가락여자 – **천운영** Chopstick Woman-**Cheon Un-yeong**
75 아직 일어나지 않은 일 – **김미월** What Has Yet to Happen-**Kim Mi-wol**

바이링궐 에디션 한국 대표 소설 set 6

운명 Fate

76 언니를 놓치다 – **이경자** Losing a Sister-**Lee Kyung-ja**
77 아들 – **윤정모** Father and Son-**Yoon Jung-mo**
78 명두 – **구효서** Relics-**Ku Hyo-seo**
79 모독 – **조세희** Insult-**Cho Se-hui**
80 화요일의 강 – **손홍규** Tuesday River-**Son Hong-gyu**

미의 사제들 Aesthetic Priests

81 고수 – **이외수** Grand Master-**Lee Oisoo**
82 말을 찾아서 – **이순원** Looking for a Horse-**Lee Soon-won**
83 상춘곡 – **윤대녕** Song of Everlasting Spring-**Youn Dae-nyeong**
84 삭매와 자미 – **김별아** Sakmae and Jami-**Kim Byeol-ah**
85 저만치 혼자서 – **김훈** Alone Over There-**Kim Hoon**

식민지의 벌거벗은 자들 The Naked in the Colony

86 감자 – **김동인** Potatoes-**Kim Tong-in**
87 운수 좋은 날 – **현진건** A Lucky Day-**Hyŏn Chin'gŏn**
88 탈출기 – **최서해** Escape-**Ch'oe So-hae**
89 과도기 – **한설야** Transition-**Han Seol-ya**
90 지하촌 – **강경애** The Underground Village-**Kang Kyŏng-ae**

바이링궐 에디션 한국 대표 소설 set 7

백치가 된 식민지 지식인 Colonial Intellectuals Turned "Idiots"

91 날개 – **이상** Wings-**Yi Sang**
92 김 강사와 T 교수 – **유진오** Lecturer Kim and Professor T-**Chin-O Yu**
93 소설가 구보씨의 일일 – **박태원** A Day in the Life of Kubo the Novelist-**Pak Taewon**
94 비 오는 길 – **최명익** Walking in the Rain-**Ch'oe Myŏngik**
95 빛 속에 – **김사량** Into the Light-**Kim Sa-ryang**

한국의 잃어버린 얼굴 Traditional Korea's Lost Faces

해방 전후(前後) Before and After Liberation

전후(戰後) Korea After the Korean War

K-픽션 시리즈 | Korean Fiction Series

〈K-픽션〉 시리즈는 한국문학의 젊은 상상력입니다. 최근 발표된 가장 우수하고 흥미로운 작품을 엄선하여 출간하는 〈K-픽션〉은 한국문학의 생생한 현장을 국내외 독자들과 실시간으로 공유하고자 기획되었습니다. 〈바이링궐 에디션 한국 대표 소설〉 시리즈를 통해 검증된 탁월한 번역진이 참여하여 원작의 재미와 품격을 최대한 살린 〈K-픽션〉 시리즈는 매 계절마다 새로운 작품을 선보입니다.

001 버핏과의 저녁 식사-박민규 Dinner with Buffett-Park Min-gyu
002 아르판-박형서 Arpan-Park hyoung su
003 애드벌룬-손보미 Hot Air Balloon-Son Bo-mi
004 나의 클린트 이스트우드-오한기 My Clint Eastwood-Oh Han-ki
005 이베리아의 전갈-최민우 Dishonored-Choi Min-woo
006 양의 미래-황정은 Kong's Garden-Hwang Jung-eun
007 대니-윤이형 Danny-Yun I-hyeong
008 퇴근-천명관 Homecoming-Cheon Myeong-kwan
009 옥화-금희 Ok-hwa-Geum Hee
010 시차-백수린 Time Difference-Baik Sou linne
011 올드 맨 리버-이장욱 Old Man River-Lee Jang-wook
012 권순찬과 착한 사람들-이기호 Kwon Sun-chan and Nice People-Lee Ki-ho
013 알바생 자르기-장강명 Fired-Chang Kang-myoung
014 어디로 가고 싶으신가요-김애란 Where Would You Like To Go?-Kim Ae-ran
015 세상에서 가장 비싼 소설-김민정 The World's Most Expensive Novel-Kim Min-jung
016 체스의 모든 것-김금희 Everything About Chess-Kim Keum-hee
017 할로윈-정한아 Halloween-Chung Han-ah
018 그 여름-최은영 The Summer-Choi Eunyoung
019 어느 피씨주의자의 종생기-구병모 The Story of P.C.-Gu Byeong-mo
020 모르는 영역-권여선 An Unknown Realm-Kwon Yeo-sun
021 4월의 눈-손원평 April Snow-Sohn Won-pyung
022 서우-강화길 Seo-u-Kang Hwa-gil
023 가출-조남주 Run Away-Cho Nam-joo
024 연애의 감정학-백영옥 How to Break Up Like a Winner-Baek Young-ok
025 창모-우다영 Chang-mo-Woo Da-young
026 검은 방-정지아 The Black Room-Jeong Ji-a
027 도쿄의 마야-장류진 Maya in Tokyo-Jang Ryu-jin
028 홀리데이 홈-편혜영 Holiday Home-Pyun Hye-young
029 해피 투게더-서장원 Happy Together-Seo Jang-won
030 골드러시-서수진 Gold Rush-Seo Su-jin
031 당신이 보고 싶어하는 세상-장강명 The World You Want to See-Chang Kang-myoung
032 지난밤 내 꿈에-정한아 Last Night, In My Dream-Chung Han-ah
Special 휴가중인 시체-김중혁 Corpse on Vacation-Kim Jung-hyuk
Special 사파에서-방현석 Love in Sa Pa-Bang Hyeon-seok